BeWilDe

MUDDLED MAZE

WIGGLE VILLAGE

SLIPPERY SLOPE

FARTREE

MARSH

WITCH'S HOUSE

A Boggle at BeWILDerwood

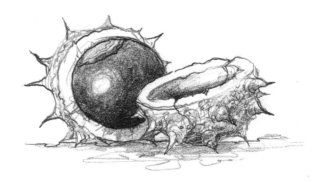

A Boggle at BeWILDerwood

TOM BLOFELD

Illustrated by
STEVE PEARCE

HOLLY DAY & BUMP PUBLISHING

First published in 2007 by
Holly Day & Bump Publishing
BeWILDerwood, Horning Road, Hoveton
Norwich NR12 8JE
www.BeWILDerwood.co.uk
Reprinted 2011

This revised edition published 2010
Copyright © Tom Blofeld 2007, 2010

ISBN   978 0 95555 430 8

A catalogue record for this book
is available from the British Library

Typeset in Great Britain by Antony Gray
Printed and Bound in China

10

Dedicated to
Larry and Leslie
without whom, etc.

The Scary Lake

Swampy was a marsh Boggle. He lived with his mum in the pretty Boggle village set deep in the reeds and the bulrushes, and went almost everywhere by boat which he pushed about with a long pole. Swampy loved his house in the friendly village in the heart of Bewilderwood and didn't often leave it. As long as there was a delicious supply of squishy marsh things for him to eat and the other Boggles didn't win too often at games like Bogglebutt, he was just fine at home.

Boggles are fun-loving creatures and they are constantly making up games but their very favourite game is Bogglebutt. This is a game where everybody stands on one leg and has to make up jokes. If nobody laughs, you have to lift up the other leg. Then you have to eat some mud stew. Swampy wasn't brilliant at Bogglebutt. In fact – between you and me – Swampy was the worst in the village.

After a morning practicing with all the other young Boggles for their annual sports day, Swampy lost once again at Bogglebutt.

Mud stew might be terribly good for growing Boggles but it

tastes as nasty as it sounds. He shivered as he looked at his grey slimy bowlful. It was going cold. So he decided to go out in his boat instead.

He gathered together a delicious snack of sedge shoots and acorns and pushed the boat out silently through the reeds and twigs until he reached the main waterway to the fishing grounds. The bubbles were bursting ploppily and the air was rich with pongy, marshy smells.

Swampy loved this place.

He found his willow rod in the boat, tied on a spider's thread and settled down to wait for a bite. While his float was bobbing in the water, Swampy began to think.

First, he thought about why he always lost at Bogglebutt. Mostly, because he told the same joke every game – about the Boggle who said he liked slugbug soup and then had to eat a whole cauldron of it – because his mother had told him that joke. She had always laughed when she told it. His mother also told him a few other things as well, like not to eat the spoon (or the bowl) at dinner-time. She had taught him to add some slitherigrubs to his mud stew to make it taste a tiny bit better.

Most importantly, she had told him, 'We Boggles don't ever go to the big Scary Lake. We never go further than the fishing puddles.' Then she tickled him and pointed out, 'A Boggle like you makes quite enough trouble just staying at home.'

After a while he began thinking that his mum's joke might not be that good after all. Perhaps … maybe … he shouldn't worry about the other stuff she had told him, either.

While he was pondering all this he suddenly had an idea, a very un-Swampy-like idea.

Now, there are two things to know about Boggles. They are not very good at ideas and they never go exploring. Today seemed different. Swampy wasn't catching fish and he definitely didn't want to go back to finish his mud stew quite yet. So he untied his fishing rod and used the pole to turn his boat gently towards the opening to the big Scary Lake.

'I reckon there's nothing big or scary about it,' he thought. 'My mum's just saying that because she's never been there. I ought to go and have a good look. Then she'll look silly.'

He steered his boat through the overhanging twigs by the alder flowers into the Outer Puddlereach. With each push, he began to feel braver and braver. He noticed that the reeds

were thinning and as he poled gently around the water-lily flowers, a sudden burst of light broke through and he saw the huge lake stretch out in front of him like a shimmering ocean.

'Goodness me, it's big,' he thought. Swampy decided first to look at it all from the edge of the lake for a while. After a few minutes doing that he took a deep breath and announced to himself, 'Right. Here goes.' A little while after that he nosed his boat slowly out into the wide water.

He stuck to the edge when he could, although he sometimes had to steer away from the frisky coots, who often played tipping games with Boggle boats. He felt terribly brave and quite important. 'No one has ever been this far before,' he thought triumphantly. 'I'm sure of it. I might actually be the bravest Boggle there has ever been. In fact, I bet . . . What was that?'

He listened hard, then heard it again – a sort of '*slish*-ing' sound and some spitting noises.

To begin with the sound was quite far away, but it was not the sort of sound an exploring Boggle really likes to hear. After a short while the sound stopped.

Just as he was nearly home, at the dyke, he heard an enormous bellow from behind him, and in a whirl of arms and legs he shot into the peaceful dark dyke, as the creature (if that's what it was) grunted horribly.

As he slipped his boat into the safe pools near the trees he heard a great trumpeted '*Blaaaaathtt*' noise on the edge of the lake. With his heart thumping and bumping he guided his boat back to his village as quickly and as silently as he could.

The Boggle Village*

'That was a great, greedy Scrunch Boggle I should say. Terribly fond of Boggles your size,' stated a Head Boggle.

'No, no, no! It's the great Sludge Vortex exploding,' interrupted another. 'I heard that'll throw your boat right over the trees.'

'Never. 'Twas a shoal of Muddleteeth ready to bite, of that I'd be sure,' mused an elderly pipe-chewer.

They all started debating which it was when Swampy's mum said, 'Well as far as I'm concerned, whatever it was, you are a very silly Boggle, but I'm glad you're safe now. Let's go back and I'll make us both a delicious tea.'

'Not till we've heard more,' cried the other Boggles in unison and Swampy, who was feeling a little better, realised that all the villagers were listening to him properly for the very first time. So he told the whole story again just in case he had left anything out.

As he was wondering if he might try out his joke again, a pretty young Boggle, who Swampy had never dared talk to before, came in carrying a huge basket of flosberries.

Now, as Boggles think more important things come first, all

the villagers stopped listening and gathered about for a bite or three. She smiled shyly as she offered the delicious berries to Swampy.

Later, as Swampy was going home for the night, with his mother holding him firmly by the right ear, the pretty young Boggle leaned over and asked in an admiring whisper, 'Did you really go all the way to the big Scary Lake?' And try as he might to feel naughty, a sort of warm glow followed him all the way home. He really had gone to the big Scary Lake.

The next morning Swampy got up and dressed in his battered spare hat, as he couldn't find his favourite one. Then, after a huge breakfast of fried fudgecake with flosberries, he set off down the plank to go fishing.

'Now remember dear, no exploring today,' said his mother.

'I know. We Boggles don't do exploring,' agreed Swampy, wearily.

'Nor having ideas neither, dearie. That's for daring folk like the Wood Twiggles and such, not for the likes of us. Now we'd like a nice sprat and some slipperfish for our supper, so you'd best be off.' She gave him a fond kiss goodbye.

It was one of those dappled sunny days when all the fish bite even if you have forgotten your bait, and Swampy had a full basket of fish before he knew it. So he put his rod down, leaned back and started dreaming about the nice, pretty Boggle; how brave he'd been and how he hadn't really been so very scared.

In a little while Swampy had forgotten everything about his mum's advice. He began to mull over all the exciting things that had happened yesterday. That, of course, is how Boggles – and everyone else – start to get ideas. So, soon Swampy had one too. 'I wonder if I should go and see my cousin, Moss, at the Wood Twiggle's village. He might know who it was who made all that noise yesterday.' He pondered some more and decided it was an excellent idea.

'How silly to think that we Boggles don't have ideas! That's the second one I've had in as many days,' he thought to himself. 'Maybe having ideas is something I'm especially good at.'

The next thing he knew, he was poling off through the scented marsh on his way to the Twiggle village in the forest.

The Twiggle Village

It isn't very far to the beautiful glade where the Twiggle tribe live, but Boggles don't go there very often. For one thing, it is all alarmingly dry and, for another, the food is a bit odd. Twiggles eat barkicrisps, airbugs and delicacies of that sort. They don't really like the squelchy muddy food that makes a Boggle's party such fun to attend. Also Boggles really don't climb all that well.

The Twiggles live high among the branches and what they like to do most of all is to dance. Not many Boggles can keep up with artfully whirling Twiggles. The Boggle habit of standing on their heads and kicking their legs in the air when the music goes too fast is considered by the Twiggles to be a little too rustic.

But Boggles and Twiggles are closely related and, on the whole, very fond of each other. Once in a while one of the villages holds a party and everybody comes along.

Some time ago, at just such a party, Swampy's Boggle cousin, Moss, had fallen in love with a beautiful Twiggle called Leaflette and they had got married and gone to live in the Twiggle village.

They were playing with their children up in the trees when they saw Swampy coming through the wood. He was looking up nervously and using his hat to mop his brow.

Moss came down and gave Swampy a few lessons in the etiquette of shinning-up trees, but it still took Swampy a long time to reach the main village platform, high in the branches. When he got there he sat very much in the middle and hugged the tree very hard. Every now and again though, he nervously peered down.

A very young Twiggle called Sticklenose was cuddled up next to him, fast asleep in Swampy's hat.

The villagers gathered round and, after clearing his throat a few times, Swampy began to tell his story of the trip to the big Scary Lake and how brave he had been. Everyone listened carefully. Then they  made up a dance of the water-jets, trailing green and red chiffon scarves, as they scampered around the branches to illustrate the best bits.

When everyone settled down they began to discuss the matter, but it was soon clear that they didn't know what had made the noise either. They made some helpful suggestions though.

'Why not go back and make it do it again? We could do a dance in the nearby trees to distract it,' suggested a Twiggle.

'But it might eat me next time,' said Swampy, after some thought.

'That's alright, we've got a dance for that too,' offered the Twiggle. This seemed to Swampy not at all the sort of plan he had hoped for.

'We could tickle it, if we could see its tummy,' suggested a small Twiggle, before hiding behind her scarf and subsiding into heaps of giggles.

It was explained that she had drunk one too many giggle spells which the witch had given them for their last party.

'A witch?' said Swampy nervously. 'Is she about here? Actually it might be a good idea if I was getting back soon. Lots to do at home you know.'

He made another cautious peek over the platform and hugged the tree a bit harder.

'But what about finding out what made that noise?' asked Moss, adding, 'Anyway, she's a good witch.'

'She knows everything about the woods and she's got a sweet little pet robin that follows her everywhere,' explained the giggling Twiggle, before collapsing into fits again.

'That is not a bad point she just made, you know,' said Moss. 'If we really want to know about all this, we could do worse than ask the witch. She really does know all about the woods.'

Swampy looked very dubious about going off to talk to a witch all on his own, so Moss suggested, 'We could go together. You, me and Leaflette. It would be a big adventure.'

Swampy felt quite sure his mum would say that if Boggles shouldn't go exploring, then they probably wouldn't like adventures. But he kept quiet, partly because he did want to find things out and also he secretly hoped the pretty Boggle might tell him again how brave he was. Also, the height was making him dizzy and he didn't much feel like talking right then.

Once the other villagers agreed to look after Moss and Leaflette's children, and Leaflette had packed food for the journey, they were all ready to go. So after everyone had been hugged and kissed goodbye, the three of them headed off down the rope-ladders to go adventuring.

Leaflette then had to flit off to find soothing herbs for Swampy's bruises, after he had found that going down trees was just as hard as going up them. In a while they were heading on their way through the gentle brown leaves of the forest floor.

'How do we get to where the Witch lives?' asked Swampy, hoping it wasn't too far.

'We have to go through the Piney Woods, over the Bumpy Hills and then we have to look for her in the Black Marsh,' said Leaflette airily.

'Oh,' said Swampy, trying to look reassured.

'If we don't get caught by a Thornyclod first,' said Moss ominously.

Swampy heard a gulping sound, then realised it was him. 'A Thornyclod?' he said, doing his best to keep the wobble out of his voice.

He was just about to mention home and how maybe it was time to be going, when a loud thud behind him made him jump.

Then a deep voice from the darkest part of the wood said, 'Boots, boots. Oh bother boots!'

The
Thornyclod

Boggles are not brilliant at climbing trees. In fact, they don't so much climb trees as fall heavily out of them. So it was with some surprise that Swampy found he had scrambled up to quite a high branch and was now looking anxiously around him. Next to him was Moss. Both their hearts were thumping.

'I think that might be a Thornyclod,' whispered Moss nervously. 'I hope they can't climb trees.'

They both sat in silence for a bit. Below them in the woods something large was clumping about in the deep undergrowth.

Leaflette called over to them from a nearby tree. 'I think I can see something down there. I'll just pop over to have a look.'

She flitted elegantly through the high branches and disappeared.

Then she called over. 'I think it is a Thornyclod. It's quite big.'

'Is it going away?' asked two not-very-brave Boggle voices in unison.

'No, I don't think it is. It's doing a sort of dance in a circle,' said Leaflette, 'and it's chanting something.'

At that moment a giant spider wearing some leaves pinned on its thorny back emerged slowly out of the gloom. It was turning around in a slow, clumpy way, making 'Ooh!' 'Ahh!' 'Eee!' 'Oh!' noises. It looked rather fierce and frightening and it seemed to be waving at the Boggles.

'I think it's spotted us. What should we do?' asked Swampy.

'Don't know.' Moss said helpfully.

They looked down at the great beast for a while.

'I don't think it's going to go away just now,' said Moss. 'Perhaps we'll both have to sleep up here.'

Swampy remembered laughing at the Bogglebutt joke about the Boggle who tried to sleep in a tree. He decided that it wasn't really all that funny when you thought about it properly.

At that moment the Thornyclod spoke. 'Hey,' it said gruffly, 'would you odd-looking Twiggles mind helping me?'

It waved a leg with an old boot on it at them.

'We're Boggles up here,' said Swampy. 'I suppose Boggles are probably not much use to you. Not if you want a Twiggle.'

'Boggles eh? Then what on earth are you doing up in the trees. You had better climb down.'

'Will you eat us if we do?' asked Moss in his best not-too-squeaky voice.

'Well,' said the Thornyclod, 'I might. Then again I might not.'

It thought for a moment before announcing, 'I certainly won't eat you if you promise to do something for me.'

They started to climb down carefully and, two bumps later, both Boggles were on the forest floor. Leaflette slipped across and joined them.

'Boggles in the trees. Whatever next,' muttered the Thornyclod.

The three brave travellers inched their way forward.

'Good afternoon,' they said.

'Not really,' grumbled the Thornyclod in a gloomy voice. 'And do you know why? Because things just aren't made properly anymore. Not at all. I mean look at this for bad workmanship. Terrible!' It waved one of its legs again. On its foot was an old boot with a flapping sole.

Now that they were closer, Swampy couldn't help noticing that the Thornyclod was wearing a different sort of shoe on each foot. Some were boots, some were wellies and one was a pink high-heeled shoe. There was even a football boot.

'Boots,' moaned the Thornyclod, 'are the bane of my life. Too many feet, too many feet.'

It thought for a while and announced, 'As you look like nice little Boggles I've decided I'll let you pass through this time, but to get back you'll have to promise to bring me a new shoe. I don't mind what sort, because they look better when they're mixed you know. And no holes! This one has holes, you see.' It waggled a leg airily. 'Makes my feet tickle.'

It put its foot down and then did another slow circle dance, exclaiming, 'Ooh! Ah! Ooh!' at each step.

As there didn't seem much choice, the Boggles promised the Thornyclod that they would bring back another shoe.

'Good! You'd better not try coming back this way without one as I'm feeling very fierce today,' warned the Thornyclod but added, 'I would look rather fetching in tap-dancing shoes, I think. I have always suspected I might turn out to be very good at tap-dancing. Or an embroidered slipper. I never had one of them. But I suppose anything without holes would do. You can give it to me on your way back.'

It clumped off slowly.

When it had gone, Leaflette suggested to the others, 'I remember the witch telling us stories about the boots on the FarTree. Perhaps she'd tell us where to find it.'

'I hope she does,' said Moss. 'Or we may have to sleep in her house till we find a boot.'

Sleeping in the witch's house with all those broomsticks and scary things seemed worse to Swampy than being eaten by a Thornyclod, and the FarTree sounded miles away.

He didn't say anything, but he made a mental note to remind himself later that sensible Boggles would be much happier if they didn't go adventuring.

The Witch

The Piney Woods weren't as dark as all that and the Bumpy Hills were hilly and no worse.

Soon they reached the Black Marsh. The tangled bushes and thorns looked impassable, even for a bog dweller like Swampy. Somewhere through the murky undergrowth he could just make out a black cauldron with a wisp of steam oozing gently over the top. There was a peculiar rich muddy smell, which actually made him feel quite a bit better.

'I don't know how we'd find anyone in there,' he commented to Leaflette.

'But there's a doorbell,' she pointed out. 'Well ... really a door-pull,' she added smiling. She tugged on a snaky vine and they heard an eerie clang ring out deep in the marsh.

'The witch's home looks a bit scary to me,' worried Swampy. 'Are you sure she's really as nice as all that? She won't turn us all into Picklenewts or something, will she?'

'Not if you're nice to her she won't,' said Moss, 'but I think she does know some frightening potions. Beyond here are the Black Tangles and she has to make sure that all the nasty things there behave themselves. Even we Twiggles never go beyond here. Something in there makes weird howling noises at night.'

Swampy found himself shivering slightly and everything seemed to go a bit quieter.

Suddenly there was a sort of flicker and a wisp of smoke and a rosy-faced witch wearing homely colourful clothes was standing right in front of them. She was carrying a delicious basket of fruit.

'Good morning, Moss,' said the witch.

'Good morning. I hope we're not bothering you,' replied Moss.

'Not at all. I've just finished brewing a tricky potion, so this is a good time to come, thank you, Moss. How nice that you've brought someone to see me.'

The witch welcomed Swampy, who did his best to grin back nervously.

'I see Leaflette and Rosie are already friends,' she smiled and Swampy turned round to see Leaflette stroking a friendly little robin which had jumped on her shoulder. The bird was rubbing its cheek against Leaflette's ear and twittering cheerfully.

'So tell me why you have come. I'll not be giving you Twiggles any more giggle powder if that's what you want. Not until that sweet little girl is better,' the witch warned the Twiggles.

'I think she thought it was sherbet,' explained Leaflette.

'It is sherbet, mostly. With a little something I add, but you mustn't let anyone take so much next time,' warned the witch looking just a little fierce. They all looked a bit nervous at that. 'Well, let's sit down and you can tell me why you have come to

see me,' the witch said kindly, pointing to a little clearing nearby with log seats. She offered the three travellers some fruit and they all sat down to eat.

When they had finished the apples and Swampy had eaten a pear, some flosberries, an orange and another small pear, they settled down to tell their stories of the big Scary Lake and the Thornyclod. Rosie the Robin hopped about twittering gaily while the Witch pondered the matter. After a while she spoke.

'I can tell you the way to the FarTree so you can get a boot,' she said, 'but you'll have to find out for yourselves what was in that lake. I know someone who can help you and I'll tell you the way there. I must warn you it's quite a long way and a bit dangerous too. But if you really need to find out, the Old Man of the Marshes would certainly know.'

Swampy was so pleased that the Thornyclod would have its boot that he forgot to be worried about the danger. He offered the witch a couple of his freshest slipperfish in gratitude. She smiled and took them gingerly, holding them at arm's length by their tails, saying, 'Delicious. These will make a lovely treat for Scrop. He's getting a bit long in the tooth to go fishing these days.'

No one wanted to ask who (or what) Scrop was.

The three explorers were given directions to the Deep Reeds. 'Go and find the Old Man of the Marshes,' the witch suggested. 'He knows everything about that lake. And if you're going, you can pick me some Swamp Lupins while you're there, the pretty white ones. I'll need them for the next giggle dance.'

'Of course we will,' said Leaflette.

'If we don't get eaten by a Thornyclod on the way,' pointed out Swampy.

'You won't get eaten by a Thornyclod,' laughed the witch.'They only eat dried leaves and twigs. They're not as fierce as they pretend. All the same, if you've made a promise to it, you'd better keep it. Now I've got some business in the Slimy Grove so I'll wish you well.' And in another shimmer, she was off.

'I never believed the Thornyclod, anyway,' lied Swampy to the others, as they set off in search of the FarTree.

The FarTree

The FarTree isn't that difficult to find. What you do is look out for paths with signposts saying 'To FarTree' and then follow them.

When Swampy and his friends got there, they saw a perfectly normal tree, only hanging off it were all types of footwear. Some were boots, some were shoes, some were slippers and smallest of all were little woollen bootees in pink and blue for the baby rabbits.

There was a purple wellington boot which Leaflette thought might suit the Thornyclod and she also pointed out a lilac dancing shoe.

Moss and Leaflette looked at Swampy in a funny sort of way and Leaflette suggested he picked them both.

'We'll give the Thornyclod a choice,' she said.

'No trouble,' he said, and he marched up to the tree.

Just as he was reaching for the boot, a huge noise went '*phhrrrpppp*' and a terrible smell filled the air.

Swampy jumped. 'What was that?' he gasped.

'Well,' said Moss, trying not to smile too much, 'did you notice that it wasn't all that far to the FarTree?'

'I did notice that. I thought it funny but . . . ' Then Swampy began to smile too. 'Ahhh . . . it's that sort of a FarTree.'

They all laughed, and Swampy laughed so much he took quite a long time to pick off the other shoe.

The Muddled ★ Maze

'We had better go and find the Thornyclod,' suggested Moss.

'I think it will find us,' said Leaflette. 'We are going to have to go near its lair if we follow the directions we were given.'

They tied the boot and the dancing shoe to Swampy's pole and set off down a narrow winding path through some chestnut trees.

Moss began singing a Boggle walking-song and they all joined in at the loud bits. As Boggle songs are mostly loud bits, they made a very noisy group as they marched along, with Leaflette dancing in time to the beat.

Moss and Swampy stopped to pick some chestnuts because a wise Boggle knows that a snack can always come in handy.

This part of the wood had lots of signs to guide travellers. Helpful instructions like 'This Way' and 'That Way' were written on the signs, and less useful ones, such as 'Probably Not Over There' and 'The Wrong Way'.

Finally they came across an arrow pointing straight up. On it was written 'The Slippery Slope'. This was what they were looking for.

In front of them was a huge gnarled tree by a very steep bank. It was so knobbly there were lots of places to put feet and hands. Even the Boggles found it very easy to climb. At the top they saw a very long branch curving down over the other side of the high bank, all the way to the ground. It had a groove cut from one end to the other. There were two more signs. One was marked 'The Fun Way', and it pointed at the branch, and the other read 'The Very Uncomfortable Way', which pointed straight down the tree trunk.

'I think I'll go the fun way,' said Leaflette, 'but you have to do it right though. The witch told me how to do it.'

Leaflette picked up a large leaf and, placing it right at the top of the grooved branch, sat down on it and pushed. She shot off along the branch at tremendous speed, shouting with pleasure. Moss was next, waving his arms and whooping. Then came Swampy. He got a bit mixed up when he pushed off, so he did it backwards.

'It's the best way for Boggles to slide,' he claimed. 'If you can't see what's coming next then it isn't so scary.'

Moss decided he would like to have another go, but it wasn't at all easy to go back up the tree. So the three travellers reluctantly pressed on through the woods towards the Thornyclod's lair.

The road wound its way on with the verges getting higher and higher. There were now hedges on each side of the paths, made from dried reeds. There were an awful lot of paths which went off in all directions.

'I must say they do like putting signs about here,' Swampy commented. 'I mean, who would write one like that?' He pointed to a post with a lot of different directions on it, saying things like 'Lost – This Way' and 'Not Sure' and 'Perhaps Not'.

It wasn't easy to decide which route to choose as each path they went down had more paths leading off from it. It seemed to be a sort of maze. The signposts kept on just saying things like 'I Doubt It' and 'Probably Not Down Here'.

Moss proposed using the old country trick of leaving a marker at

each turning. 'We could use the chestnuts as a trail. That way we'll know if we have been here before and if we get stuck we can always find our way back,' he suggested.

Each turn made things more confusing and after a while they all began to feel very lost. Then Leaflette suddenly stopped. She put a finger to her lips. 'Shhh, I think I can hear something moving about, just round that corner,' she whispered.

They listened and heard a rustling sound mixed in with squelchy noises.

'Look there! There are hundreds of different footprints on

the ground. Whatever it is there seem to
be a lot of them.' Leaflette sounded
worried.

'I don't want to meet that many
creatures at once,' said Moss, 'they
might not be friendly. We had better go back the
way we came. Thank goodness we marked the way back.'

The others agreed with him but when they looked for
the chestnuts, they had all gone. Leaflette was just about to
suggest that whatever had made the footprints had probably
taken the nuts, when she saw Swampy shuffling away making
swallowing noises.

'We weren't supposed to eat those, Swampy,' scolded Leaflette.

Swampy went very red. 'I'm sorry, I forgot. Chestnuts are
my favourite sort of nuts, you see.' He looked very ashamed
but there wasn't a lot they could do about it now, so Moss
suggested another plan. 'I think we must be brave and go and
meet whoever's round the corner. We'll have to hope they
know the way out.'

'What if they want to eat us?' protested Swampy.

'Well, at least you'll be chestnut-flavoured,' said Moss, without all that much sympathy.

Swampy looked so guilty now that Moss did something really
courageous. He offered to go and look first.

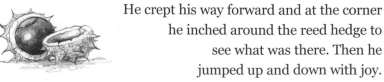

He crept his way forward and at the corner
he inched around the reed hedge to
see what was there. Then he
jumped up and down with joy.

Lunch in the ★ Lair

'It's alright everyone. It's only the Thornyclod. That's who made the footprints.'

The Thornyclod turned round and saw them. 'My Goodness, it's the tree-Boggles! How did you find your way in here?' It asked, looking very worried. 'I put so much work into making all those confusing signs and paths, so nobody would find my lair.'

'We've brought you a boot,' said Leaflette, producing the purple wellie, but the Thornyclod didn't seem all that interested. In fact, it seemed to be hiding something behind its back.

It tried to look fierce and commanding.

'Right then,' it said gruffly, 'I won't have to eat you as you've brought me a boot, so you can all go.' It gestured the way out with at least two of its feet. But Swampy didn't move.

'You wouldn't have eaten us anyway,' he accused. 'We found out you don't eat Boggles. The witch told us you only ever eat leaves and moss and things.'

'Oh! She said that, did she? Well I suppose I don't really eat Boggles. Just my little joke, really! Now off you go.' The

Thornyclod was backing away from the three of them. It seemed to be trying to hide a saucepan which was bubbling away in the corner.

'What's that delicious smelling stuff there in your pot?' Leaflette asked, pointing to the pan behind the Thornyclod.

'Oh you wouldn't like that. Just a marshmallow mixture. For Thornyclods only. Not good for Boggles. Really, I'm only learning how to cook.' The Thornyclod looked evasive.

'I'm a Twiggle, not a Boggle, and I'm sure I'd like marshmallows,' Leaflette stated.

'I bet we would too, and we're Boggles,' said Swampy, licking his lips thoughtfully.

The Thornyclod sighed. 'I suppose you'd better have a very little bite then.' Then it suggested hopefully, 'Perhaps you'd prefer an oakleaf sandwich instead? Those are very good and I could make one up in a second, with an acorn dressing if you like.'

'No. We'd prefer the marshmallows,' said three voices at once.

It turned out that there was an awful lot of the mixture. Leaflette showed the Thornyclod how to use leaves to wrap up the little sweets. They were too hot to eat right away though. So while they waited for them to cool down they gave the Thornyclod the purple boot and the ballet shoe. It was delighted with them.

'I'll keep the dancing shoe for a special day if I may. Though I must say, you have excellent taste in footwear. Quite the thing this boot and just the right colour too. Goes with my eyes don't you think?'

The Thornyclod did a little dance and didn't make tickled noises once. It tried some of the barkicrisps, which it pronounced to be the most delicious food it had ever tasted. Leaflette gave it the recipe. 'You can come to our next party, if you want. There are bound to be lots of other things to eat that you might like,' she offered. The Thornyclod looked very pleased.

'I'd be delighted to attend and I'll cook something for it as well.'

'We should be going now because it will take us ages to find our way out,' said Swampy gloomily.

'You can use my special route if you want,' suggested the Thornyclod, kindly.

It showed them to a stairway which wound its way up one of the trees.

'There's a rope bridge up there, and when you get across you'll be on the path to the Dark Woods. I hear they lead to the Deep Reeds but I've never been there. Good luck, my little friends. It was very nice to meet you.' It gave each of them a marshmallow in thanks for the boot.

The three friends crossed the bridge in silence and set off along the road to the Dark Woods. After quite a while Moss spoke. '*Ecshellent* marshmarrows these.'

'*Delishus.* Bit chewy though,' agreed Swampy, picking at his teeth with a twig.

'*Mmmmnnnmm Mnnnn,*' said Leaflette, trying to unglue her teeth with both hands.

Sticky or not they tasted very good.

46

The Dark Woods

A great many paths lead to the Deep Reeds and some are longer than others. It was a part of the wood which was lovely. Yellow flowers were bursting from below the bushes under the shady light of the great trees, and the pretty green ferns were full of Bluefrill butterflies which were so tame that the travellers could let them sit on their hands. Moss whistled a Boggle song and Leaflette and Swampy sang along jauntily. Even the birds seemed to be twittering to the happy tune.

In a while however, the trees began to loom taller and taller and the path became darker and gloomier. Swampy noticed that there weren't any signs out here and there were an awful lot of turns. After a while he asked, 'Are we all sure this is the right way?'

'No,' Moss replied, 'I'm not. Maybe we should have gone left down the last path.'

'Ah,' said Swampy.

'I'm not even sure I could find my way back now,' said Leaflette.

'Oh,' said Swampy.

After that the conversation thinned out a bit.

They continued walking for what seemed like hours, then stopped for lunch by a pretty holly tree where Leaflette produced food for all of them from her bag. Not only that, but she had even remembered to bring some Sweetsludge Pie which Boggles love. Moss and Swampy cut a huge slice and then Swampy had another one. Leaflette ate some Honeytwigs with a slice of Barkbread. After this they all felt much better.

It was Moss's idea to climb the trees to make sure they were going in the right direction. 'Just look where the sun is and if that's always to our left, we'll be near enough right,' he said.

Swampy and Leaflette said that they thought they knew what he meant.

After the first few accidents, they decided to appoint Leaflette the tree climber.

Except for a couple of wrong turns she guided them further and further through the dark woods. Instead of the pretty butterflies, now there were large black birds making harsh screeching noises in the dense treetops. Once, something huge lumbered through the undergrowth right by them but it didn't stop. The air felt a little chillier.

Just as Swampy was getting worried that they would never find their way through the forest, he suddenly smelt a slight hint of a marshy pong in the air again.

Now, all Boggles know that where there is marsh, there will be reeds. 'My nose tells me we are getting closer,' he said to Moss.

'Mine too. But how are we going to get through that?' Moss pointed to an enormous thicket of spiny bushes right in their way.

'I'll climb up and have a look over it,' called out Leaflette and she disappeared up a very tall tree.

'I can see right across from here,' she shouted down to the others, 'but I can't see how to get there.'

On the ground, Swampy and Moss searched in the bushes but no one could find a gap. The thorny branches were too thick and spiky. Just as he had almost given up hope Swampy noticed something odd on a huge tree half covered in ivy. When he cleared it, he found a forgotten, battered old sign. What the sign had originally said was 'The New Bridge' but someone had crossed out the word 'New' and written 'Broken' instead.

Underneath that, on a really scruffy bit of wood, were the words 'Be . . . Bats', with a picture of an arrow pointing straight up.

Moss was the first to speak. 'It must be a joke,' he supposed. 'I do feel a little bats coming this far into the Dark Woods.'

Leaflette climbed up to investigate. After a while she called down from the top branches.

'I've found a bridge; it's all the way up here in the treetop.

You'll have to climb a long way up, though. I'll throw down an ivy creeper to help pull you up.'

It was not one of those tree climbs, though, where everyone has a fun time. Somehow neither Boggle fell off and Swampy had the bright idea of using his pole to help pull Moss up, and then things became much easier. Even so, they were very out of breath when they got to the highest branches. And, at the end of one of these branches was a bridge.

It was made of wood and rope with ancient creaking boards, and it stretched all the way above the thorny thicket to the top of another very tall tree. It was a long way on the other side. They stood and gazed at it nervously until Leaflette said, 'Well it won't get any easier if we just keep looking at it.'

'We've come this far,' ventured Swampy, 'so we might just as well go on.' But it took a little time before Leaflette bravely took the first step.

The old wooden slats creaked, but they held. They all edged very slowly along with each board sounding like it was just about to crack under their feet. Above their heads some very dark birds seemed to be hovering.

Suddenly Leaflette stopped. 'Oh dear!' she said, 'I don't think that sign was meant to be funny after all.'

Looking over her shoulder, the others saw what she meant. In the middle of the bridge was a big hole and on the other side, a pile of wooden planks which someone had brought to mend the bridge, but they hadn't done it yet. There was no way across.

The Broken Bridge

'I've got a bad feeling,' said Moss. 'I don't think that sign meant to say "Be Bats" at all. Perhaps it once said "Beware of Bats", only the middle broke off. Look over there!' He pointed a shaky finger to the sky.

They stared at what had seemed to be small black birds but they were circling nearer now, and they began to look much larger. The three realised that they were, in fact, huge bats with very sharp, nasty looking teeth. They circled above the small travellers.

Close up they seemed big enough to carry off anything but the very tubbiest Boggle. More of them were gathering in the tree at the start of the bridge.

'We're trapped!' Moss cried. 'What should we do now?'

The menacing black swarm was swooping lower.

No one answered. Then Swampy had another one of his ideas, a very un-Boggle-like big idea. He looked at the others and muttered, 'I hope this works,' and before they could stop him, he ran straight towards the gap in the bridge. He was holding his pole right at the end and to the others' amazement, he dug one end into the last rotten board and in a graceful arc, vaulted over the gap. He flew high across the broken section and landed with a thump.

It was just like Boggle Sports Day.

As he landed, the wooden board he had vaulted from crumbled and little fragments went tumbling and turning all the way down to the dark forest far below.

'Wow', he gasped. 'I made it. Gosh!' He fought an urge to lie down.

Swampy dragged the planks on the other side into place, and a few moments later Leaflette, Swampy and Moss were on the far side of the bridge, and then they were all running like crazy to the end. The bats wheeled off disappointed and flew back into the trees.

'Goodness, that was scary,' said Leaflette, panting heavily.

Moss looked at Swampy in admiration. 'That was the bravest thing I ever saw a Boggle do,' he said.

Swampy found that he was shaking quite a lot and, as he looked back at the broken bridge, he wondered how on earth he'd done it.

But he had.

It would have been another bumpy climb down for the Boggles, but Leaflette thought of a much better way.

There was a long rope keeping the bridge up which stretched all the way down to the ground. She broke off a forked twig for each of them.

'We can slide down,' she said. 'You've just got to jump. Watch me.'

She looped the twig over the rope, held both ends and jumped off, whizzing down the rope shouting with excitement.

The two Boggles weren't quite as keen when it was their turn but even Swampy enjoyed it and both agreed it was a much better way of getting down than just falling out of the tree.

So they set off again on their travels to the edge of the Deep Reeds.

The Deep Reeds

It felt good to be in the open swamps again with the gentle sunshine warming the reeds. Beautiful pink and green birds were chattering away in the small trees which were dotted about. Long tufts of grass waved gently in the breeze.

They journeyed past the reeds and bulrushes and very soon found the pool that the witch had told them about. It was a shaded pretty place with yellow and blue irises around the edge and in the middle of the pool was a large mound covered in grassy white flowers, but The Old Man of the Marshes didn't seem to be home.

They stopped and rested on some tussocks of sedge and considered what to do next.

'Let's just wait for him to come home,' suggested Moss. 'It's nice here,' and he stretched out in the dappled sunshine with his pack tucked under his head.

'What do we call him when he does come home, though?' Swampy wondered out loud. 'We can't just say "Old Man", can we?'

'Do what I always do if you're not sure and just call him "Mr",' said Leaflette.

Swampy said he generally mumbled a guess into his shirt if he forgot someone's name. Moss said he just 'ummed' or 'erred' until he could ask a friend.

'But who could we ask out here?' Swampy pointed out.

At that moment a deep resonant voice suggested, 'You could always ask me.'

'It's The Old Man of the Marshes. He's back,' cried Swampy, looking about everywhere.

'Just as you say,' replied the rich voice. Each time he spoke, the ground rumbled a little.

'We thought you might have another name?' suggested Leaflette nervously.

'No need when there is only me,' the voice answered. 'Of course, my mother used to call me "Squidgy", but that was a long time ago – a very long time ago indeed. Hmmm . . . yes . . . Long, long ago.' The voice became deeper and sleepier and it sounded like he might be about to take a nap.

Suddenly he seemed to wake up again. 'But where are my manners? Welcome to my humble home, welcome to all of you.'

'Thank you,' said Moss. 'It is lovely. Just one thing though, I can't see you.'

'Yes you can, right in front of you. I'm taking my bath,' and the big flowery mound in the middle of the pond opened a huge eye and gave the three a very slow wink.

Swampy gave a big grin as he realised that the mound with flowers growing on it was the head of The Old Man of the Marshes, just poking out of the water.

'Excuse me if I don't get up,' said the voice from the water.

'Only I do like a long bath. Last year I had one for the whole summer, but this year I've lost my loofah. Now tell me, why have you come to see me?'

Swampy told his story about the thing in the lake which had scared him so much. He liked people listening to him tell the story, so he even included the part about his mum's Bogglebutt joke.

Swampy and Leaflette groaned out loud, but to Swampy's surprise the marshy ground wobbled and trembled as the Old Man slowly chuckled to himself. 'Slugbug soup Eh? I remember that one. Rather a favourite in my day.'

'So, I suppose you want to find out about the noise in the lake,' he said, after a while.

'Yes please.'

'Alright, I'll tell you how to find out. You'll need to go back to the lake. It's not far past those bulrushes.' The deep voice drifted to a halt.

'And then?' they asked excitedly.

'And then? Ah yes. Go to the edge and wait there. Then just see what happens.'

'See what happens?' Swampy asked. 'Is that all?'

'Yes. That should sort you out I think.'

'Oh,' said Swampy a little gloomily, adding quickly, 'I mean, thank you.'

'No trouble at all,' said The Old Man of the Marshes. 'I always like to help. You'd better pick the witch some of my flowers. They're the ones she likes, I believe.'

While the other two walked over to the bulrushes, Leaflette bent down and gently picked a few flowers from the Old Man's brow. As she turned to go, she patted his great forehead and said quietly, 'Goodbye Old Man. Thank you so much.'

A deeply contented rumble gently filled the air.

Meeting ★ Mildred

Not far past the bulrushes turned out to be true in a way. The lake was quite close really, but every time one of them found a path, a fallen log or an impenetrable bit of marsh was in the way.

As they pushed through, they each tried different routes and were soon separated, although they could still hear each other, especially Moss, who seemed to be plunging through hedges of spiny plants.

The last thing Swampy heard him say was, 'Rose bushes are only nice from the outside. Must remember that.' Then Swampy was carefully crossing a very thin branch to get over a muddy water hole. The branch broke just as he made it across.

He finally reached the water's edge more exhausted than nervous and when he got there, instead of remembering to be frightened by the monster, he just sat down to mop his brow. Suddenly it happened again – the *shlishing* noise, the turmoil of waves and the great jets of water.

Swampy dived back into the bushes for cover. Whatever the thing was, it now was noisily splashing about in one of the channels in the marsh. With his heart thumping, Swampy cautiously parted the leafy branches and could just make out his friends right across the other side of a muddy pool, but he was cut off from them. The broken branch meant that he couldn't go back. He stayed in the bush to think.

He wondered to himself if being munched by Muggleteeth was going to hurt much. He decided it probably would.

He could hear his mum saying in her kindly voice, 'Boggles don't have ideas and Boggles don't go exploring.' He wished he'd listened to her.

And then he saw the monster. It was zooming about the lake in rapid zig-zags and it was very long, with a great spiky back. Not only that, it had teeth. A lot of teeth! And while it was diving about, it was making a strange noise, 'Yoo Hoo! Yoo Hoo!'

It stopped its mad chasing about and began to swim lazily right in his direction. It had seen him. 'So this is it,' thought Swampy to himself. 'I'm going to be eaten up like a ripe stinkapple.' He closed his eyes tightly and waited for the end.

The creature came closer and closer. Swampy could hear it stop just by the bush where he was hiding. Any moment now he would be gobbled up. He hoped Boggles tasted nasty.

He sat there shivering for quite a long time, but nothing happened. He decided he might have a tiny peek out of the bush, through his hands.

To his amazement, a great cheesy smile rose out of the water attached to an enormous pair of eyes.

'Hello, *Itth* you again,' said the smile. 'I shouted to you *latht* time but maybe you didn't hear me. I'm Mildred.'

Swampy just stared, unable to speak.

'Hello again,' said Mildred brightly. 'I'm a Crocklebog. I come from a long line of Crocklebog*th*. Other Crocklebog*th* . . . like me,' she explained. 'Ooh look, a duck! A duck!' Then, without further conversation she plunged off after it. The duck flew away startled.

'Yoo Hoo!' Mildred shouted excitedly after the disappearing bird. Then it was gone. 'Bla*th*t. I'll never get a friend, never!'

She swam back. '*Th*orry to *th*artle you la*th*t time, only *th*omeone put thi*th* up my no*the*.' She produced a battered hat which Swampy recognised as his own. 'It made me *th*peak funny and I've already got a li*th*p.'

Finally Swampy spoke. 'Hello,' he said.

'Would you like to be friend*th* with me,' asked Mildred, hopefully. 'I do try hard to make friend*th*, but I don't have many. Probably becau*th* I've got a li*th*p and . . . Ooh a butterfly. A butterfly!' and Mildred was off again giving chase. She came slowly back. 'Hopele*th*. Hople*th*. I try *th*o hard to make friend*th* with them but . . . Oh well.'

'Perhaps it's because you frighten everyone,' suggested Swampy.

'Me? Frightening? No, never. Not me. I even like flie*th* and thing*th*. I'm a vegetarian,' she announced proudly.

'You scared me before,' said Swampy. 'Springing up at me like that.'

'Oh,' said Mildred, looking crestfallen, 'i*th* *th*pringing bad?'

'Ye*th*,' said Swampy, 'I mean yes.'

'I'm *th*orry.' She looked miserable.

'But the lisp is nice though. Friendly,' said Swampy, to cheer her up.

64

The effect was almost immediate. 'Ex*th*ellent. I won't worry about that anymore.'

Her attention was distracted for a moment by a coot, but Swampy got his next question in before she shot off. 'Are you really vegetarian?' Mildred nodded energetically.

'And you don't eat Boggles?'

'*Yeauch*!' said Mildred. 'I like fruit though, c*th*ccially gluberrie*th*. And I like a *th*ludgecurrent or two. Oh, and pear*th* and pongipea*th* and orange*th* and ooh, what do you call tho*th* yellow little berrie*th* with white *th*po*th*?'

'Slozzleberries,' suggested Swampy.

'I like them too,' said Mildred, licking her lips thoughtfully.

'My mum has lots at home. They're yummy.' It was getting late in the day so Swampy thought it was time to move the conversation on a bit.

'I wonder, could you help me and my friends. We need to get home and it's on the other side of the lake?'

'*Th*imple,' said Mildred. 'Hop on my back.'

A few moments later a very surprised Moss and Leaflette saw the extraordinary sight of Swampy riding an enormous Crocklebog towards them.

'We can get a ride home with Mildred,' he shouted to them. 'Only bring some reeds for us to sit on as it's a bit thorny up here.'

'I come from a long line of thorny Crocklebog*th*,' announced Mildred to the others. 'Hardly any *th*mooth one*th* at all, though they're very friendly too. Crocklebog*th* are friendly, but mainly thorny,' she concluded.

'Ah,' said Moss and Leaflette, at the same time.

They fetched the reeds and had a lovely swishy ride across the lake.

When they got there, Swampy asked, 'Would you like to come to supper with me and my mum? We could bring things down to the water if you like.'

'But I'm not wearing going out clothe*th*,' said Mildred. 'I couldn't po*th*ibly meet anyone without them.'

'Well, we're having a giggle party next week. You could come to that,' suggested Leaflette. '*Th*ertainly, I'll come to that,' agreed Mildred, adding, 'I will look lovely.'

So the three friends went back to the Boggle village where Swampy's mum cooked all the fish that Swampy hadn't dropped or lost in the marshes. She even found some Barkicrisps for Leaflette. They were the tiniest bit stale but still delicious.

Then they drank hot Swillipond and watched the sun go slowly down through the trees.

The Big Party

Soon it was the day of the party. The little giggling Twiggle was still giggling, but it turned out that she was just like that. Even when Swampy told her his joke she giggled, but Swampy decided that as he had so many better stories now he wouldn't tell it again.

Everyone wanted to hear the tale of their adventures and the Thornyclod waved its new smart boot when that part of the tale came around.

It hadn't seemed that Moss and Leaflette had done all that much, the way Swampy told the tale, but they were having such a lovely time with all their friends that they didn't mind.

The witch announced that as everyone was so happy, she wouldn't let them have any giggle powder this time but told them all to save it for a really grey day.

Just as the Boggles were settling down to eat their flutterfloss and pink midgibuns, there came a terrible *whooshing* sound and two great arcs of water flew all the way over the village.

Everyone went quiet.

'Oop*th. Th*orry,' called out Mildred. 'Am I late?' She was

wearing the tiniest tiara of sparkling stones on her head and clutching a gold lame handbag.

'Not at all,' said Moss. 'Now that everyone is here we can really start to have fun.'

And they did.

The Twiggles flew about like ballerinas and the Boggles stood on their heads and waggled their legs like mad. The chirping birds feasted on the delicious cake crumbs and even the little rabbits brought their babies along. Everyone in Bewilderwood was having fun.

Just when Swampy thought it couldn't get any better, he

heard a pretty Boggle voice whisper to him, 'I think you were so brave,' and Swampy turned to the nicest girl he thought he had ever seen and said, 'Would you like to dance? We could stand on our heads together if you want.'

But they didn't, and they danced properly all night.

The End